KNIGHTS OF RIGHT

Also by M'Lin Rowley

Knights of Right, book 1: *The Falcon Shield*
Knights of Right, book 2: *The Silver Coat*
Knights of Right, book 3: *The Warrior's Guard*

Visit us at ShadowMountain.com

Library of Congress Cataloging-in-Publication Data

Rowley, M'Lin.
The fiery gloves / M'Lin Rowley.
    p. cm. — (Knights of right ; bk. 4)
  Summary: Joseph, Ben, and Sam must complete still another quest to prove their ability to choose correctly and get the next piece of armor, as they work to become Knights of the Round Table.
  ISBN 978-1-60641-241-1 (paperbound)
  [1. Knights and knighthood—Fiction. 2. Stealing—Fiction. 3. Conduct of life—Fiction. 4. Arthur, King—Fiction.] I. Title.
  PZ7.R79834Fi 2010
  [Fic]—dc22   2009049216

Printed in the United States of America
R. R. Donnelley, Crawfordsville, IN

10 9 8 7 6 5 4 3 2 1

KNIGHTS OF RIGHT

BOOK 4
THE FIERY GLOVES

M'LIN ROWLEY

ILLUSTRATED BY MICHAEL WALTON

SHADOW
MOUNTAIN

1

COUNTING CANDY

"If you give me five pieces of chocolate, I'll give you all five of my red-hot fireballs," Ben offered, holding up the candies.

Joseph shook his head, searching through the pile of his candy on the tree house floor.

"No, thanks," he said, pulling out some candy corns for True Heart. The falcon was crazy about them. When Joseph ripped open the package and scattered them on the ground, True Heart screeched and began picking them up with his beak like a chicken. Joseph and Ben laughed.

"Why won't you trade? I'm being fair—five for five, right?" Ben protested.

"Because I'm almost out of chocolate and I don't like fireballs that much."

"But you have so much candy that five pieces of chocolate won't make much of a difference," Ben countered, trying to make a puppy dog face. "I'm sick of fireballs, and they're all I have left!"

"You ate *all* your candy?" Joseph exclaimed.

"Yeah, and it's the second week of November, too! This is the longest I've ever managed to make my Halloween candy last. You should be proud of me!" Ben smiled.

Joseph shook his head in disbelief. He scooped his candy protectively into his plastic pumpkin.

"No deal. You should have saved more," Joseph said. "Do you realize it's been two weeks since we last saw King Arthur? I wish he would summon us. I would much rather face another quest than do homework."

The brothers had met King Arthur that summer in the woods behind their home. He had traveled forward in time to make them knights of his Round Table. As the boys made good choices and passed different tests, they earned pieces of armor that helped them fight the Black Knight and his evil friends. So far they had faced a troll and a pack of werewolves. Joseph could only imagine what they might have to fight next. He looked at the tree house wall where hung the shields, chain mail, and breastplates that he, Ben, and Samantha had earned so far.

That armor would have made great Halloween costumes, thought Joseph. It was too bad that only he, Ben, and Sam could actually see it.

Sitting next to the armor were King Arthur's crown and scepter. The legendary king had let Joseph borrow them to wear on Halloween when the Black Knight would have more power. They didn't see any sign of the Black Knight while they were trick-or-treating, but Joseph was proud of his costume even if the crown was a little too big for him. He laughed when everyone told him he looked like a real king. If only they knew how real his costume was!

Now he was anxious to return the crown and the scepter to King Arthur. He didn't think King Arthur needed them, since Ben and Joseph and Sam seemed to be his only subjects in the modern world. Still, Joseph would feel better when King Arthur had them back.

"Why don't we go into the woods to see King Arthur, Joseph?" Ben asked, hopefully. "What if the troll escaped? Maybe he couldn't get the werewolves under control. We'd better check!"

"You know King Arthur told us not to come back until it was time for the next quest. T. H. will let us know when we're to go. Anyway, I have to get this homework finished. It's due before Thanksgiving break."

"No, wait! How about this? You give me four chocolates for five fireballs! Come on, you have to admit it's an awesome deal!" Ben pleaded.

Joseph shook his head again.

"Then how about three chocolates for five fireballs? It's almost like you're doubling your candy! I'm losing a lot!"

"I said no," Joseph said as he climbed down the ladder.

Ben sighed. He shoved his yucky fireballs back into his coat pocket and grabbed a candy corn from the floor before True Heart could get it. The falcon squawked and flapped around Ben's head, pecking at his hair as Ben laughed and climbed down the ladder after Joseph.

2

SLUDGE SOUP

The boys were working on their homework at the kitchen table when True Heart flew up to the window. The falcon tapped persistently on the glass with his beak just below the picture of a turkey Katie had made in preschool. She told her brothers she'd named the turkey after the falcon and insisted that their mom tape the picture to the window.

"Look! T. T. and T. T.! Two T. T.'s!" Katie pointed excitedly.

"Good counting, Katie," their mom said.

Joseph stifled the urge to remind Katie that the falcon's nickname was T. H., not T. T.

"Mom, that's the signal! Can we go? " Ben jumped up.

Mom nodded, and the boys hurried out into the backyard to grab their armor from the tree house. Then True Heart led them over the fence and into the snowy woods.

"Katie's turkey looks nothing like a falcon," Joseph complained. "T. H. is too cool to have a turkey named after him."

"Actually, I don't think Katie's turkey looks much like a turkey. It looks more like a pool of brown sludge," Ben said. "Good thing Mom doesn't make brown sludge for Thanksgiving dinner, huh, Joseph?"

"Whoa, look at that," Joseph said instead of answering. Through an opening in the trees they could see a big black cook pot hanging from a support made of three large tree limbs. Steam was rising from the pot, and the last coals of a dying fire glowed beneath it.

"I wonder who would make soup way out here," Joseph said.

"I can think of somebody—this is probably the Black Knight's camp! Let's go spy on him!" Ben said, running forward.

"Ben!" Joseph whispered loudly. "Come back!"

When Ben didn't stop, Joseph sighed and ran after him. Someday Ben would learn not to snoop around asking for trouble. But apparently today wasn't that day.

The boys quietly moved closer to what seemed to be a campsite in a small clearing.

There were two tents near the cook pot and fire. If one of the tents belonged to the Black Knight, Joseph hated to think about who slept in the other tent. It looked too small for the troll. He didn't think werewolves slept in tents, so maybe the Black Knight had recruited someone else to fight against King Arthur and his knights.

The camp seemed deserted, though the fire was still smoking. Joseph didn't think anyone would be in the tents in the middle of the day, but the camp gave him the creeps. The sooner they left and made their way to the castle, the happier he would feel. Of course, he rarely got his way when it came to his younger brother. Sure enough, Ben had to poke around the campsite before they left.

"Look at this," Ben whispered, pointing to

a strange medallion hanging above the cook pot.

"Cool. Now let's go," Joseph whispered back, anxiously looking around. The Black Knight had a bad habit of sneaking up on them.

"Look! There's soup in the pot," said Ben excitedly, even if he was still whispering. "Too bad it isn't chicken noodle. It looks like—ha! It looks like Katie's picture! Brown sludge! We should add some dirt or something and see if he notices. That'd be funny!"

"I'm sure it would, but we have to go." Joseph tugged on his brother's arm. "We need to see what King Arthur wants, and I need to give him back his scepter and crown."

"Fine, fine," Ben grumbled under his breath. "Maybe later."

But before Ben followed his brother back into the woods, he stopped and tilted his head as if he'd heard something.

Joseph had seen True Heart do that, but when Ben did it, it just looked funny. He smiled and started to say something, but Ben put a finger to his lips and pointed at the bigger of the two tents.

Ben crept toward it and peeked under the tent flap. In the darkness he could see someone's back. It was a man chanting something. He was pretty creepy sounding, and Ben gulped. This must be the Black Knight!

Suddenly the man stopped chanting and turned his head toward the tent flap.

With a yelp Ben stumbled backward, but his foot caught on the edge of the tent. The tent collapsed in a jumble of fabric and sticks as he scrambled to get away.

Ben and Joseph ran as fast as they could through the woods toward the castle, glad the Black Knight was trapped in his tent without his armor or crossbow.

"What was that all about?" Joseph gasped as they hid near the castle while Fidelis let down the drawbridge.

"The Black Knight was chanting something creepy. I think it was a spell," Ben said confidently. "In fact, I know it was a spell. I'll bet he's collecting more followers right now."

Joseph gulped. "A spell? Knights can't do magic, can they?"

"Who knows!" said Ben. "The guy must be pretty bored if all he has to do all day is cook soup and chant. He should take up playing video games or something."

"We'd better see what King Arthur thinks."

"About video games? Do you think King Arthur would want to play some with us?"

"I meant about the spell, Ben." Joseph rolled his eyes.

By that time Fidelis, King Arthur's dog, had lowered the drawbridge, and the boys followed him into the throne room, talking more excitedly now that they were safe in the castle.

"I still think we should've added something to his soup while he was in his tent," Ben sighed.

"Maybe you should have tossed your fireballs into it." Joseph grinned.

"And get nothing for them? No way!" Ben

15

shook his head. "I'm going to get some choc-olate—or at least a sucker—for them. I have to."

"I guess it doesn't hurt to keep trying." Joseph smiled. "Just don't keep trying me. I won't give you a peanut."

"Half a peanut that you sucked on first?"

"Sick! No way!"

3

OLD LEGENDS

"Hey, Your Majesty!" Ben called. "Fido looks great!"

"Yes, Fidelis is almost completely recovered." King Arthur smiled as the boys approached the throne.

As if he understood, Fidelis barked happily and chased his tail in a circle in front of them. Ben and Joseph laughed.

"And how are you boys doing?" asked the king.

"We're fine," Joseph answered. "Thank you for letting me borrow your crown and scepter, Your Majesty. It was an awesome Halloween. The magic must have worked because we didn't see any sign of the Black Knight while we were trick-or-treating."

He handed the sack containing the crown and scepter back to King Arthur.

"But we did see the Black Knight today," Joseph continued. "I think we found his camp in the woods. Ben says he saw him performing some kind of spell. What do you think?"

King Arthur frowned and rubbed his chin. "I think that is very possible."

"You mean the Black Knight can do magic?" Joseph gulped.

"He has a bad kind of magic. It is powerful, but it will never match good magic," King Arthur explained. "Still, we must be on our guard. The Black Knight is cunning, and if Ben is correct, we'll have more of his allies to deal with very soon."

"If that's true, we'd better get started on our next quest."

King Arthur nodded. "Very good. And I have another story for you, if you would like to sit down. It is one of my favorites."

"Yes! A story!" Ben exclaimed as he lay back on the floor in front of King Arthur, using Fidelis as a pillow.

"Once upon a time there was a knight named Sir Matthew. He was journeying in the mountains far from home when he fell through a crevice into an underground cave.

"This was not a simple bear's den or animal lair. This cave belonged to a tribe of dwarves who, fortunately for Sir Matthew, were absent at the time.

"Because climbing back up through the crevice was impossible, the knight searched for another way out. He went deeper and deeper into the cave, until finally he came to a small carved door.

"Beyond the door the knight found himself in a large room full of amazing treasures created by the dwarves in their underground world.

"Dwarves are famous for their craftsmanship. Their swords are the finest in the world. But if a dwarf sword is acquired dishonestly, that sword will be a curse rather than a blessing.

"Sir Matthew knew this legend and was

not tempted to pick up any of the magnificent blades he passed.

"But at the far end of the chamber was a large chest filled with beautiful jewelry of every kind. Now Sir Matthew was in love with a young maiden, and he desired to impress her with tales of bravery and conquest. He chose a golden necklace from the hundreds in the chest and left the chamber to find his way back to the surface.

"In time he returned home from his journey and presented the token to his love. Sadly, when she put on the chain, it tightened around her neck and instantly choked her to death."

"Oh!" said Ben. "That is horrible!"

"Your stories are definitely rated PG,

Your Majesty," said Joseph. "They're pretty violent."

"If PG means Perfectly Good at helping young boys learn the consequences of their behavior, then I accept the term," King Arthur told them. "The wisest people learn from the mistakes of others."

"You don't have to worry about us giving girls any deadly jewelry, Your Majesty," Ben joked.

"I hope not, Benjamin. I am counting on you to make other good choices as well. Be safe and be wise on your next quest, my young knights!" King Arthur called as they left.

Fidelis followed them out of the castle. "See you later, Fido!" shouted Ben. "We're so glad you recovered from the werewolf attack. Be on your guard for more bad guys, okay?"

Fidelis barked back as he raised the drawbridge behind them.

"Let's hope your yelling didn't attract the Black Knight or any more of those bad guys you were warning Fidelis about," Joseph said anxiously.

"You worry too much," laughed Ben. "I'll race you home. Remember Dad said that he would take us out for hamburgers today?"

4

STUCK

Ben excitedly tore the wrapping from his burger as soon as he sat down at the table. They hardly ever ate fast food, because Dad was a doctor and didn't really believe in it. Joseph popped some fries into his mouth and grinned.

"Thanks for lunch, Mom and Dad," Joseph said.

"You're welcome," his dad said, but he looked puzzled. He was looking at the receipt in the bag and counting the burgers. "Uh-oh.

They gave us an extra burger. I didn't pay for this one."

He held up the burger for everyone to see.

"Free burger! Hip, hip, hooray!" Ben laughed. "Ha, ha! Too bad for them."

"Ben," Joseph groaned. "That's not very nice."

"Joseph's right. It's not honest. I need to go back and pay for this," Dad said. He grabbed the car keys and hurried out to the garage just as True Heart hopped over to Ben and tried to nibble a bite of his burger.

"Hey!" Ben swiped away his burger.

"Share, Benny! Share!" Katie said. "T. T.'s hungry!"

"Hungry? He has all the birdseed he could ever want back in his birdhouse. Birdseed, T. H.! Birdseed!" Ben exclaimed.

True Heart squawked and watched them finish eating.

After lunch Ben sat in Joseph's room, waiting for his brother to finish writing a book report. Joseph had promised to help Ben build a snow fort as soon as he was finished.

True Heart flew in and dropped a pair of handcuffs into Ben's lap.

"Hey, cool! I forgot we had these!" Ben said excitedly, picking them up.

Before Joseph knew what was happening, Ben had handcuffed his brother's wrist to the bed.

Joseph tried to yank his hand away. "Ben!" he groaned. "Now look what you did! Get me out of here!"

"If I had a piece of chocolate, I might be willing to help you out," Ben grinned.

Joseph gave him a withering look. "Do you want help with the snow fort?" he asked.

"Okay! Okay!" Ben laughed. "I hope T. H. knows where to find the key!"

First True Heart led Ben to the tree house. There the falcon found another candy corn but no key. Then True Heart led him to the fridge and sat on the counter squawking until Ben got him a drink of water. Still no key. Then they went back outside, where True Heart chased down a mouse and ate it.

"Yuck! You're just hungry, aren't you?" Ben groaned. "I give up." He walked back into the house and up to the bedroom.

"No key?" Joseph asked.

"T. H. just led me on a wild goose chase!" Ben said. "Or more like a wild mouse chase."

"What?" Joseph asked. "And you're just giving up!"

"Uh, of course not! I just came to see how you were doing." Ben shook his head and tried not to look guilty.

True Heart landed on his shoulder.

"Well, uh, look, T. H.," said Ben, "since Joseph hasn't found out how to get free by himself, you and I better get back to work. Come on, my friend, let's find that key and save Joseph so we can make a snow fort!"

They hurried out of the room. True Heart led him downstairs to the drawer in the kitchen that was full of all kinds of stuff. The family called it their junk drawer, because that's exactly what it had in it. Ben made a face when he opened it. Someone had left the lid off the glue bottle, and glue had spilled all over the drawer.

"The key better be in here, T. H.," Ben said. He dug through the goop but couldn't find any trace of the key. All he got was glue-covered fingers. Everything he touched stuck to him, and then his hands stuck to his shirt when he tried to wipe them off.

"No luck. And I really am giving up this time," Ben sighed when he got back to Joseph's room.

Joseph did not look happy. Three-year-old Katie had

found Joseph handcuffed to his bed and set up a tea party to help her big brother feel better.

"Wanna play tea party too, Benny?" she asked.

Ben shook his head. "You're having too much fun for me." He grinned as he

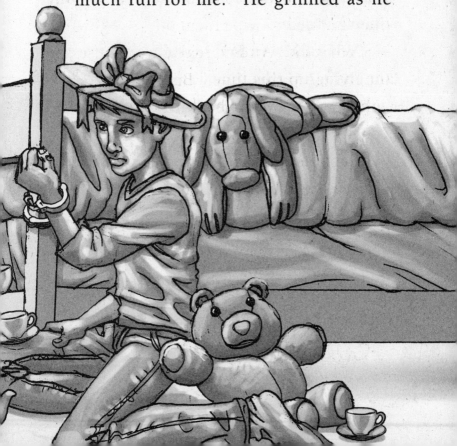

looked at the tea set and the stuffed animals on the floor by Joseph.

Joseph glared at him.

"Did you even look for it?" Joseph asked.

"Yep, and all I got was glue all over my fingers. T. H. must have lost his touch. He led me to the tree house, the fridge, and the junk drawer. No key."

"What did you find in the tree house and the fridge? Maybe they were clues too."

"Naw, T. H. was just hungry and thirsty." Ben shook his head.

"But T. H. doesn't eat glue. Maybe the glue is a clue, just like the handcuffs," Joseph said thoughtfully.

"Handcuffs and glue. What do they have in common?" Ben asked.

"Well, they both get a person stuck. What

is a bad choice that can get you stuck in life?" Joseph wondered.

"Going four-wheeling up a muddy dirt road right after a rainstorm?" Ben answered.

Joseph laughed and shook his head.

True Heart flapped into the room. He dropped the key and a small candy bar into Joseph's free hand.

"Hey! T. H. knew where the key was all along! And where did he get that chocolate? Does he have a Halloween stash I don't know about? That crazy bird!" Ben chuckled.

"Crazy bird, crazy bird, crazy bird," Katie chanted in her parrot voice.

Ben quickly unlocked the handcuffs.

"Phew! I was afraid I was going to be stuck there forever," Joseph said, rubbing his wrist.

"Maybe T. H. secretly works for Katie and that was part of her master plan," Ben suggested. "That is so evil, forcing her brother to play tea party with her!"

"Nice try, Ben. Why don't you take the clues seriously for once?"

"Good idea," Ben responded. "That candy bar T. H. gave you is a clue, too. I better take *that* and give *it* some serious thought. I do my best thinking while I'm eating."

"Not a chance!" said Joseph. "You can't eat this clue."

"Oh, well. You know I had to try. But now you're free, let's go build that snow fort."

"Nope. This whole handcuff thing took too much time," Joseph said, shaking his head. "I still have to finish my book report."

Ben sighed and leaned back against Joseph's bed.

"Tea party now, Benny?" Katie asked.

Ben quickly jumped to his feet. "No thanks, Katie," he answered as he hurried out of the room.

5

HANDS-ON TEST

Ben wandered around the backyard, kicking the snow with his boots. It wasn't fun to build a snow fort alone. Now that Joseph was in junior high, it seemed as if he was busy all the time. Ben climbed into the tree house and sat down.

Then he remembered Joseph's plastic pumpkin filled with Halloween candy. It was hidden in the chest in the corner. Ben opened the chest. It was so tempting. He could take some of Joseph's chocolate, and he wouldn't have to trade anything for it. Besides, had

Joseph counted every single piece? He might not notice any was gone. Ben dug through the pumpkin and counted out four pieces of chocolate. That should be few enough that Joseph wouldn't notice.

With a sigh, Ben tossed the candy back into the pumpkin. It wouldn't be right, and he knew it. He had to remember what a knight would do. He put the pumpkin back in the chest and turned to go.

His foot caught in a piece of chain mail that had fallen off its hook. He tripped, and his hands scraped across the rough wooden floor as he landed. Ben winced and looked at his hands, expecting them to be full of painful slivers. Instead Ben saw that his hands were protected by silver gloves that covered his arms up to the elbow. He cheered with excitement before hurrying to climb out of the tree house. He'd passed the test!

Ben ran inside, shouting excitedly. He hurried to the office, where Joseph was printing his book report.

"I did it! I did it!" Ben gave Joseph a light punch on the shoulder so his brother would notice his new gloves.

"Hey!" Joseph yelped. "Did what? Start taking karate or something?"

"No, look!"

Joseph finally looked up and saw the gloves. His mouth hung open, and Ben almost stuck a finger in it before Joseph popped it closed.

"Keep your mouth open like that and you'll catch flies!" Ben laughed.

"You had your quest already? What was

it? We'd better call Sam and tell her about the clues!" Joseph decided.

He grabbed the phone while Ben told him about his quest. Joseph didn't look happy about Ben almost taking his candy, but Ben was saved when Sam answered the phone.

They decided the handcuffs were definitely a clue, and so was the candy. Joseph thought the glue was the third clue.

"Probably is. We'd better look out for times when we're tempted to take something that isn't ours," Sam said.

Joseph agreed, and they said good-bye.

Next morning Joseph grabbed his book report and headed to his English class, wondering when his challenge would appear. Ben's earning his gloves for deciding not to steal

Joseph's Halloween candy made Joseph feel like writing King Arthur a thank-you note.

But Joseph didn't see how anything like Ben's challenge could happen to him. *I would never steal,* he thought. And he hadn't seen anything like a challenge yet. Besides, he was already tired of Ben's bragging about his gloves.

Joseph had been so busy thinking about the clues that he hadn't realized the hall was almost empty. He was going to be late for class! He hurried down the hall, almost running.

Just outside his classroom, he saw a piece of paper lying on the floor. It was a twenty-dollar bill. Twenty bucks! Joseph gasped and picked it up. *I could buy a lot with twenty dollars,* he thought excitedly. He and Ben had been saving for a long time to buy a video game. This twenty dollars would mean they could finally buy it.

Who could have dropped a twenty-dollar bill? It would be impossible to find the true owner among all the kids in his junior high. Someone dishonest might claim it, even though he hadn't dropped it in the first place. The right owner would probably never show up.

But Joseph knew it wasn't his money and he should take it to the office. He would be late to class, and he and Ben wouldn't be able to buy that video game yet, but turning in the money was the right thing to do.

Joseph walked down to the office. The secretary looked up when he came in.

"Hi, how can I help you?" she asked cheerfully.

"I found this outside my classroom," he answered, holding out the twenty-dollar bill to her. Before she could take it, the office door flew open. The breeze made the bill flutter to the floor in front of the desk.

Joseph bent down to pick up the money just as Mr. Gunther rushed into the office. They collided, and Mr. Gunther stepped down hard on Joseph's hand. He was surprised to see Mr. Gunther's shoe on top of a shiny silver glove, rather than on crushed fingers. A grin spread from ear to ear.

Joseph felt great that he had passed his challenge and won his silver gloves. He couldn't stop smiling as he left the office, even though Mr. Gunther kept apologizing

and acting worried about Joseph's hand. The assistant principal probably thought Joseph was crazy, but his hand really wasn't hurt. Just wait till he showed Ben his new gloves.

6

GAME OVER . . . ALMOST

At the store, Samantha was looking through a supply of poster board, trying to decide what size and color her group needed for their science project. Her group consisted of herself and two boys. Normally, she wouldn't have minded, but these boys were annoying. They never paid attention in class, and they had reputations as troublemakers. She had a feeling she was going to be doing the whole science project herself.

"Hey, look at these cool games," Tim said to the other boys, pointing at a glass case across the aisle from the school supplies. Inside were all the expensive video games. The door seemed to be open slightly.

"Unlocked too!" Jeff whispered excitedly. "Wouldn't it be great to have that basketball one?"

Sam ignored them and looked at her list. The only thing they still needed was rubber bands. She put her backpack on the floor so she could reach a package of them on a higher shelf.

While her back was turned, Jeff grabbed the game he wanted out of the case and slipped it into her open backpack.

"Let's go to the checkout," he said. "I think we've got everything."

Once the group was outside the store, the boys began to talk at once.

"I can't believe you did that, Jeff!" Tim exclaimed.

"I know! But really, Sam did all the work." Jeff laughed.

"What are you talking about?" Sam asked.

"Check your backpack," Jeff said.

Quickly Sam opened her backpack and pulled out the game. "What is this?" She glared at Jeff.

Tim looked away uncomfortably, but Jeff said proudly, "Awesome, huh? Maybe I'll even let a sissy girl like you play it some time."

"Nice try. I'm taking it back," Sam said firmly. She headed back to the store before Jeff could stop her.

"Don't take it back, stupid," Jeff complained. "We were lucky to get it out of there!"

Sam ignored him and hurried into the store. She didn't notice the manager following her as she walked back outside.

Just as Sam reached Jeff's car, Tim saw the manager.

"Sam told on us!" he gasped.

"What?" Sam asked. She turned around to look, her hand on the frame of the car door.

Jeff hit the gas, and the door slammed on her fingers. Sam pulled her hand back, but instead of crushed fingers, she saw shiny silver gloves. Her fingers were just fine.

Behind her the manager finished writing down the license plate number of Jeff's car. "Thank you for returning that video game, young lady. I was watching you the entire time you and your friends were in the store, so I know you weren't involved in taking it,

but I'll need your statement about what happened."

While the manager spoke to the police, Sam admired the shiny metal of the silver gloves. She smiled to herself. It might not be easy to be a knight, but it was a lot harder *not* to be one.

7

PICTURE THAT

"Say turkey!" Mom said, holding up Sam's digital camera.

Ben and Joseph looked at each other and grinned. Mom could be so corny at times. Sam, Ben, and Joseph were wearing all their armor: shields, chain mail, breastplates, and gloves.

Mom looked at them one more time and snapped the photo. Then she smiled and handed the camera back to Sam.

"Hey, our armor doesn't show up." Sam pointed at the screen.

"I'm sure King Arthur will like the picture,

anyway. You print it out, Sam, and I'll find a frame for it," Mom decided.

Sam nodded and went to the printer in Dad's office.

"Take this too! Take this too!" Katie waved a photo toward Joseph.

The boys looked at it together.

"Well, here's a picture where the costume actually shows up," Joseph said.

It was a photo of Katie and True Heart on Halloween. At the last minute, Katie had decided to be a pirate, not a princess. She kidnapped True Heart and turned him into her parrot. The two of them wore matching eye patches and red bandanas. She'd tried to paint his feathers red before Joseph saved him, but even without the paint, True Heart didn't look very happy with his little eye patch and bandana.

Joseph laughed and handed the photo back to Katie.

"T. T. looks like parrot pirate!" she told her brothers as she ran off to show Sam.

"I don't think King Arthur would like his falcon turning to piracy," Ben laughed. "We'd have to call him Black Heart or Captain Jack Falcon or something. And he'd go around stealing everyone's hamburgers and candy corns. Anyone with junk food would be doomed!"

"Oh, speaking of stealing food, thanks again for not taking my candy," Joseph said suddenly.

Ben looked at him in surprise. "No problem. And since I'm such a nice guy, how about giving me a piece of chocolate in appreciation?"

"Ben!"

"Just kidding! Just kidding!" Ben laughed as Joseph whacked him playfully with his glove.

"So what did the clues mean, anyway?" Ben asked.

"Well, it is against the law to steal, and if you do, you can go to jail," Joseph replied. "The handcuffs warned us about that. And the candy was obviously a warning to you not to take my stuff! I think that means it's wrong to take even little stuff from your family. You need to respect other people's property, no matter whose it is."

"So what about the glue?"

"People who shoplift are sometimes called sticky fingers," said Sam. She walked into the room and slid their photo into a simple frame for King Arthur. "Maybe that's what T. H. meant by the glue. I know I am never going to have sticky fingers. Those boys each have to do thirty hours of community service for their first shoplifting offense, and they have a record now. Nothing is worth that."

"Yeah, I am sure Sir Matthew's girlfriend thought the same thing," laughed Ben.

Sam looked confused.

"King Arthur's story—I forgot you didn't hear it. I'll catch you up on the way," Ben said. "Let's go!"

They all headed for the back door. The boys laughed as Sam struggled to pull on a coat over her breastplate and chain mail. Finally she just gave up and followed them out into the snow.

8

STICKY SITUATION

On their way through the forest, Ben pulled Sam aside. "Look at this," he whispered. "We think it's the Black Knight's hideout."

The three knights-in-training crept closer to the camp. It seemed deserted, but the brown sludge was still bubbling in the pot, and the Black Knight's strange medallion was still hanging over it.

"Holy Toledo! It's the necklace thingamajig I saw before," Ben exclaimed, forgetting to whisper.

"Nice name for it," Joseph muttered sarcastically. "Come on, let's get out of here. And be quiet!"

Instead, Ben reached for the medallion, accidentally hitting the stick that was holding it. The medallion fell into the pot with a plop.

"Ben!" Sam and Joseph groaned.

"Don't worry. I'll get it out!" Ben looked down into the sludge and made a face.

"What if it burns you?" Sam pointed out.

"I've got gloves." He held up his hands and wiggled his silver fingers. He stuck one hand into the soup and felt around for the medallion. At last he pulled it out and cleaned it off in some nearby snow before hanging it back on the stick.

"I was thinking about taking it," Ben said,

"but I'd just earned my gloves for not stealing. That'd be pretty stupid if I stole something two seconds later. Stealing is wrong, even if you're stealing from a bad guy."

Sam and Joseph gave Ben high fives.

"Let's get out of here," Joseph said. "This place is creepy."

True Heart squawked, and they all hurried away from the camp.

Ben was the first to spot the huge wooden contraption moving slowly through the woods to their left. The creatures pushing it were chanting. They were so short it was hard to see them through the bushes.

"What is that?" Ben asked, pointing.

"It looks like a catapult of some sort," Joseph said.

"Not *like* a catapult, Joseph. It *is* a catapult," Sam said. "And it's headed toward the castle. We have to warn King Arthur!"

"They're dwarves!" Ben yelled to Sam and Joseph, who were running down the trail ahead of him. "We don't have to hurry. They're short and slow."

One of the dwarves saw him and shouted something. The contraption started to move through the trees a lot more quickly.

"Ben!" Sam and Joseph groaned together.

The three of them ran through the forest as fast as they could to beat the dwarves and their catapult to the castle.

"Picture that thing in our backyard! Wouldn't that be sweet?" Ben called to Joseph as they ran.

"Or you could picture it launching rocks at the castle. That would not be sweet. Keep running!" Joseph shouted back.

9

DWARVES IN BATTLE

"Thank you for coming to warn me, but there isn't much we can do, I'm afraid," King Arthur sighed. "Until I get those werewolves under control, I can't use the magic for anything else."

"So the magic is running out?" Joseph asked worriedly.

"No, no. Do not worry. The magic will hold. And although an army of dwarves can be frightening, this old castle will hold as well. But I am worried about you children.

I do not want any of you getting hurt. You should hurry back home."

"We want to stay and help you!" Ben protested.

"There must be something we can do!" Joseph agreed.

King Arthur shook his head sadly.

"You haven't earned any weapons yet, and it's too dangerous to fight the dwarves unarmed," King Arthur said firmly. "It will be easy for you to sneak past them. They don't notice anything when they are using their catapult. Fidelis and I will be safe from their rocks. They'll leave when they get bored or hungry—which dwarves do quite frequently, by the way."

"We'll go, then, if you're sure you'll be all right, Your Majesty." Then Sam remembered.

"We brought you something," she said, pulling the picture out of her pocket.

"Ah, don't the three of you look wonderful in your armor," King Arthur smiled. "Isn't it wonderful to own and wear something you honestly earned and didn't steal? You will make fine knights some day."

"But I thought the armor didn't show up in the picture," Sam frowned.

"Magic!" Ben and Joseph realized at the same time. They grinned.

"Magic indeed!" King Arthur nodded. "But what do you call this type of magic?" he asked, pointing at the picture.

"It's called a photograph." Sam smiled. "Maybe I could bring my camera next time to take a picture of you and Fidelis!"

"We could show you how it works," Ben added.

"I would like that very much," Arthur agreed. "A camera that makes photo-giraffes."

"Not photo-giraffes, Your Majesty," Sam laughed. "Photographs."

King Arthur showed Ben, Joseph, and Sam a side door where they could swing across the moat away from the dwarves.

Sam was getting ready to go first when Ben shouted, "Look out!"

Out of nowhere two flaming balls as big as Ben's head soared over the drawbridge and landed in the courtyard. "Yikes! They're not launching rocks. They're launching fireballs! They're going to set the castle on fire!" Ben yelled. "What do we do?"

"We put out the fire," Sam yelled back.

The first fireball landed in a snowbank and was extinguished. But the second landed in a pile of straw, which burst into flames.

"Our gloves!" Ben realized. "I didn't get burned by the Black Knight's gross soup, so I bet they would work here too!"

The three of them reached the fire just as it spread to the door of the castle. They beat on it fearlessly with their gloves. By the time that fire was out, another fireball launched over the wall had caused a wagon to go up in flames.

King Arthur heard the noise and came out into the courtyard as they finished putting out that fire.

"You'd better stay inside, Your Majesty," Joseph called as a fireball landed in the straw near King Arthur's feet. Ben and Joseph ran to put out the flames.

"Thank you!" King Arthur sighed in relief as the fire was put out. The edge of his cloak was singed, but otherwise it was okay. "Is there some way you could use their own weapons against them?"

"Of course!" Joseph exclaimed. "Why didn't we think of it earlier?"

When the next fireball landed, Ben scooped it up in his gloves and threw it back over the wall as if it had been a football.

A gasp and an angry yell let him know the fireball had landed too close to at least one dwarf.

"A little more to the left," Sam suggested. "We want to hit the catapult more than we want to hit the dwarves."

Joseph caught the next fireball and threw it back. It was a direct hit, and a beam on the catapult started to burn. The dwarves, even with a burning catapult, tried to launch more fireballs, but every time they did, the balls came right back.

"Nice hits, you guys," Sam complimented. "You have great aim!"

Flames quickly engulfed the catapult, and the dwarves fled. The fire didn't spread to the trees because of the wet snow, but it completely destroyed the catapult.

Sam, Ben, and Joseph exchanged exhausted high fives with their silver gloves.

"Fidelis and I owe you our deepest gratitude," King Arthur smiled.

"It was no problem, Your Majesty. Glad we could help," Sam assured him.

"Remember, right makes might!" King Arthur called after them as they followed True Heart back through the woods.

10

FIREBALLS

"You want to make a snow fort with me?" Ben asked Joseph the next day.

"Not right now. I'm actually helping Sam with her science project. Her group dumped her, so I said I would help," Joseph said, gluing one Popsicle stick to another. Sam was in Dad's office, typing information to glue to the poster board.

"Eating Popsicles in the middle of November? Are you crazy?" Ben asked, looking at all the Popsicle sticks piled on the table.

"Maybe I am crazy," Joseph shrugged, "but only because I'm about to make a deal with young Benjamin Adams."

"What kind of a deal?" Ben grinned, sitting down quickly.

"Five pieces of chocolate, five fireballs," Joseph said.

"Six chocolates, five fireballs," Ben countered.

"Five for five," Joseph said firmly.

Ben held out his hand, and they shook on it. Then Ben ran to grab the fireballs out of his otherwise empty pumpkin.

"What made you change your mind?" Ben said as they made the trade. He smiled down at his chocolate.

"We need them for Sam's project," Joseph said. "We're making several models of the dwarves' catapult to see which design uses the principles of physics the best. I thought it'd be cool to launch the fireballs."

"You could build a life-sized model to put in the backyard instead," Ben suggested hopefully.

"Nice try," Joseph said. "So you could launch things all over the neighborhood? I don't think so. I don't want to be responsible for arming a short person on this side of the forest."

"Hey, I'm almost as tall as you are. And I'm much more mature than you are too!"

The next second Ben was jumping crazily around the living room, trying to catch in his mouth the fireballs Joseph launched from the catapult.

"More mature?" Joseph smiled. "Really?"

Okay, Knights of Right, let's see if you've earned your armor. King Arthur has a few questions for you . . .

1. What would you do if friends wanted to shoplift at a store?

2. What would you do if you found some money on the ground?

3. What would you do if you were tempted to take candy that belonged to a family member?

4. Why is shoplifting wrong? What are some of the consequences of shoplifting?

5. Is it ever okay to "borrow" something from a family member without asking? Is taking something that belongs to a family member stealing?

6. Why do you think King Arthur wanted the young knights to learn the importance of choosing not to take something that didn't belong to them?

7. If you had seen the Black Knight's medallion hanging by the pot, would you have been tempted to take it? Why didn't Ben take it?

8. How does taking something that doesn't belong to you make you feel?

9. How do you feel when you turn in to the appropriate authority something you've found that doesn't belong to you?

King Arthur asks—Did you know?

1. Peer pressure is one reason people shoplift. Some do it to seem cool or daring. Some do it because their friends do, and they want to be part of the group. Some shoplift because they can't afford to buy things like their classmates have.

2. Shoplifting is a serious offense. What might seem like a harmless prank can affect a person's future, including the chances of getting a job. Lots of teens find out the hard way that stores take shoplifting very seriously.

   Shoplifters may—

   - be arrested and paraded through a store in handcuffs.
   - face charges for theft.
   - be banned from stores or malls.
   - end up with a criminal record, which can make it harder to get a job, get into college, get scholarships, or do other things they want to do.
   - find that their names have been put on a national database that some companies look at when making hiring decisions.

3. People don't have to get caught for shoplifting to affect their lives. Some people may feel guilty or ashamed of what they've done. It can cost such a person self-respect or the respect of others. Sometimes people lose friends who decide they don't want to be close to someone who doesn't have the same values they do.

4. Read more at http://kidshealth.org/teen/school_jobs/good_friends/shoplifting.html

**Remember, Knights, right makes might.
Keep making good choices and
earning your armor!**

King Arthur

ABOUT THE AUTHOR

M'Lin Rowley is seventeen years old and attends American Fork High School in Utah, where her mascot is a caveman rather than a knight. She loves snow skiing, rock climbing, going to movies with her friends, and writing stories. M'Lin hopes that people will enjoy her books and learn something from them.